BIG BIRD
Joins the Carnival

by Cathi Rosenberg-Turow
Illustrated by Dennis Hockerman

Featuring Jim Henson's
Sesame Street Muppets

Inspired by SESAME STREET PRESENTS: FOLLOW THAT BIRD,
screenplay by Tony Geiss and Judy Freudberg

A SESAME STREET / GOLDEN PRESS BOOK
Published by Western Publishing Company, Inc.
in conjunction with Children's Television Workshop

"Look, Oscar! There's a carnival in town!" Big Bird said. "I think I'll ask Mr. Snuffle-upagus if he wants to go with me."

"Big Bird, you're the only one on Sesame Street who's ever seen this Mr. Snuffle-upagus," Oscar said.

"Well, why don't you come with us and see him for yourself?" asked Big Bird.

"Grouches hate carnivals," said Oscar, and he slammed down the lid of his can.

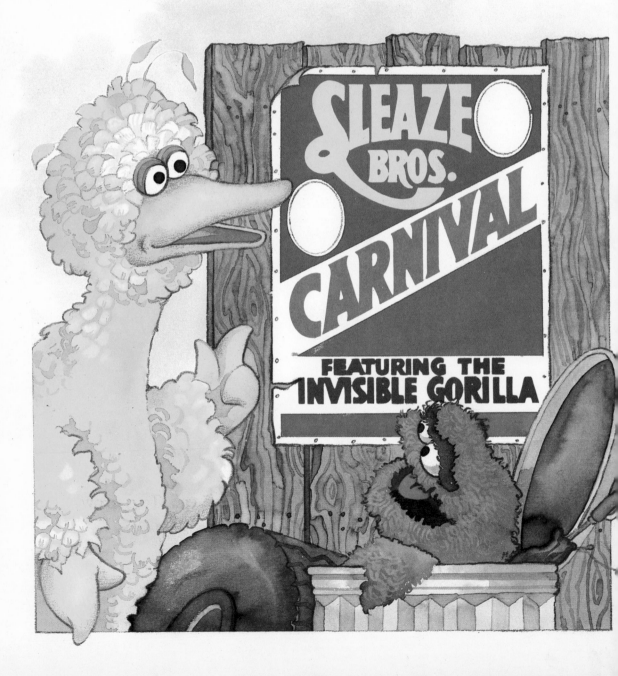

SLEAZE BROS. CARNIVAL

FEATURING THE INVISIBLE GORILLA

Big Bird walked to Snuffy's cave. "Guess what, Snuffy?"
he said. "I'm going to my very first carnival. Do you want to
come?"

"Ooooh, dear," said Snuffy. "I don't think I can. Tomorrow
is the big Snuffle-upagus hopscotch contest, and I have to
practice all day."

"You keep practicing and I'll come and tell you all about the
carnival on my way home," said Big Bird.

When Big Bird got to the carnival, he rode on the Ferris wheel.

Big Bird went to see a
fortune teller. She could look
into a crystal ball and tell Big
Bird what would happen to him
in the future. She said, "Big
Bird, when you grow up you're
going to be a big bird."

There was food at the
carnival that Big Bird had never
tasted before. He tried a candied
apple on a stick and a cloud of
pink fuzz called cotton candy.

Then Big Bird rode
around and around
on a merry-go-round.

"Step right up!" shouted a
man at a booth. "Pitch the coin
into the bottle and win a giant
teddy bear."

When the man handed him
his prize, Big Bird thought,
"Imagine! If I joined this
carnival, I could win a teddy
bear every day."

The fun house was filled with flying bats, creaking skeletons, and howling ghosts.

"If I didn't know this was make-believe, I'd be really scared," said Big Bird.

The fun house mirrors made him look like a skinny turkey
or a rubber duckie. "When I look in the mirror over my nest, I
always look the same," said Big Bird.

"Gee," said Big Bird. "This is so much fun. I wish I could come to the carnival every day."

Big Bird turned and almost bumped into two men. "Greetings, Bird," said one. "We're the Sleaze Brothers, and we think we can make your wish come true. How would you like to be in our show? You'll be the star of the carnival!"

"Me? Big Bird? A star?" Big Bird cried. "I can't wait!"

So Sam and Sid painted Big Bird blue.

"Now you've got pizazz," said Sam Sleaze. "We'll call you the Bluebird of Happiness."

SEE THE
BLUEBIRD
OF
HAPPINESS

Big Bird became the biggest star in the carnival. He sang and tap-danced all afternoon.

"Gee, if my friends on Sesame Street could only see me now," thought Big Bird.

"Thank you very much for letting me be part of the carnival," Big Bird said to the Sleaze Brothers after the show. "Now I have to go home."

"Who said anything about going home?" asked Sam Sleaze. "You're the biggest star in the carnival now."

Big Bird's beak started to quiver. "But tomorrow is Mr. Snuffle-upagus's hopscotch contest and I have to be there!" he cried.

The Sleaze Brothers pushed Big Bird into a giant birdcage.
They slammed the door and locked it with a giant key. "You'd
better get some sleep, Bird," they said. "We're leaving tomorrow
morning for Pittsburgh."

"Pittsburgh! Oh, no!" cried Big Bird.

Meanwhile, back on Sesame Street, Mr. Snuffle-upagus's feet were tired from playing hopscotch. "Ooooh, dear," he said. "I wonder where Bird is. He was supposed to come back a long time ago. I'd better make sure he's okay."

So Snuffy went to find Big Bird at the carnival.

Snuffy looked everywhere for Big Bird. Then he saw a blue
bird in a cage. "Is that you, Bird?" he asked.

"Snuffy!" Big Bird cried. "Boy, am I glad to see you!
I'm in trouble! The Sleaze Brothers locked me in this cage and
are taking me to Pittsburgh!"

"Don't be scared," said Snuffie. "I'll pull a snuffle trick and
be right back!"

Mr. Snuffle-upagus shuffled over to the Sleaze Brothers and hid behind some bales of hay. He slipped his snuffle into Sid's pocket and pulled out the key to Big Bird's cage. Then he hurried back to let Big Bird out.

Big Bird jumped out of the cage and gave Snuffy a giant hug. "You saved me!" he cried.

Snuffy just chuckled and said, "What are best friends for, Bird? I've been waiting to use my sneaky snuffle trick for a long time. Now it's getting dark, and my mommy will be worried about me. Bye, Bird."

When Big Bird finally got back to Sesame Street, Oscar popped up out of his can. "Oh, no!" he said. "It's bad enough we have that big yellow canary running around this street. But now we have a *blue* one, too. Hey, do I have a friend for you."

"Oscar!" said Big Bird. "It's me!—I've been painted blue."

So Big Bird told Oscar and Telly and Grover and Ernie and Bert all about his adventure at the carnival.

"I think you need a bath, Big Bird," said Bert.

Everyone helped wash the blue paint out of Big Bird's feathers.

"Big Bird, there is just one teensy-weensy thing about your adventure that I still do not understand," said Grover. "How did you get out of the birdcage?"

"Mr. Snuffle-upagus, of course," said Big Bird. "He used his sneaky snuffle trick to steal the key from the Sleaze Brothers and unlock the cage."

Oscar and Telly and Grover and Ernie and Bert looked at each other.

"Will you stop talking about that Mr. Snuffle-upagus," said Oscar.

"We're glad you decided not to join the carnival!" said Ernie.

ABCDEFGHIJK